Lari Don and Claire Keay

Picture Kelpies

TEA

Catriona **loved** opening birthday presents, but she **hated** writing thank you letters.

Granny said Catriona couldn't play with her new toys until she had written her name tidily at the bottom of **all** the thank you letters to **all** her aunties and uncles, and put them in **all** the right envelopes.

Catriona knew it would take

to write the thank you letters.

"Why do I have such a **LONG** name?" she asked Beanie the cat. "C-a-t-r-i-Oh, I'm **TOO TIRED** to finish this one…"

Dear Uncle Merlin,

Thank you very much
tea set. I can't wait t

Love from

Ca

For the blue-and-white
play with it.

Catriona wondered if there was a way to write her name faster.

She wrote with both hands at the same time.

That didn't work.

She piled all the letters up
and pressed really hard,
hoping she could write on
all the sheets at once.

That didn't work.

She asked Beanie to help with the envelopes and stamps.

That didn't work either.

Then Catriona remembered the big old pot under the stairs.

Granny said it was for making soup, but Catriona thought it looked like a magic cauldron.

"Beanie, let's invent a potion to bring pencils to life, so **they** can write my name for me!"

Catriona put the cauldron on the table, filled it with water, then laid her coloured pencils round it in a pretty pattern.

For the blue pencil she dropped in a bluebell,

for the red pencil she dropped in a strawberry,

for the green pencil, a handful of grass,

for the yellow pencil,
a ball of wool,

for the orange pencil,
a carton of juice,

for the pink pencil,
five glittery beads,

and for the brown pencil,
a sprinkling of earth.

“I wonder which magic words bring things to life?” Catriona asked Beanie as she stirred with Granny’s longest wooden spoon. “What about …

whiffle whiffle whoot

Poot!”

Nothing happened.

So she tossed a perfect sharpening
from each pencil into the
potion and chanted,

"Sparkly
sprinkles
and
shiny
stars!"

Nothing happened.

Ple

"I'll have to write these letters on my own, unless I find the right magic words." Then Catriona remembered what Granny and Mum agreed was ***the*** magic word.

She leant right over so her breath made ripples on the surface of the potion, and whispered, "***Please.***"

The potion swirled and bubbled.
The cauldron hopped and danced.

The spoon jumped out and dripped potion on the pencils.
The pencils twirled off the table.

Then the pencils began to write!

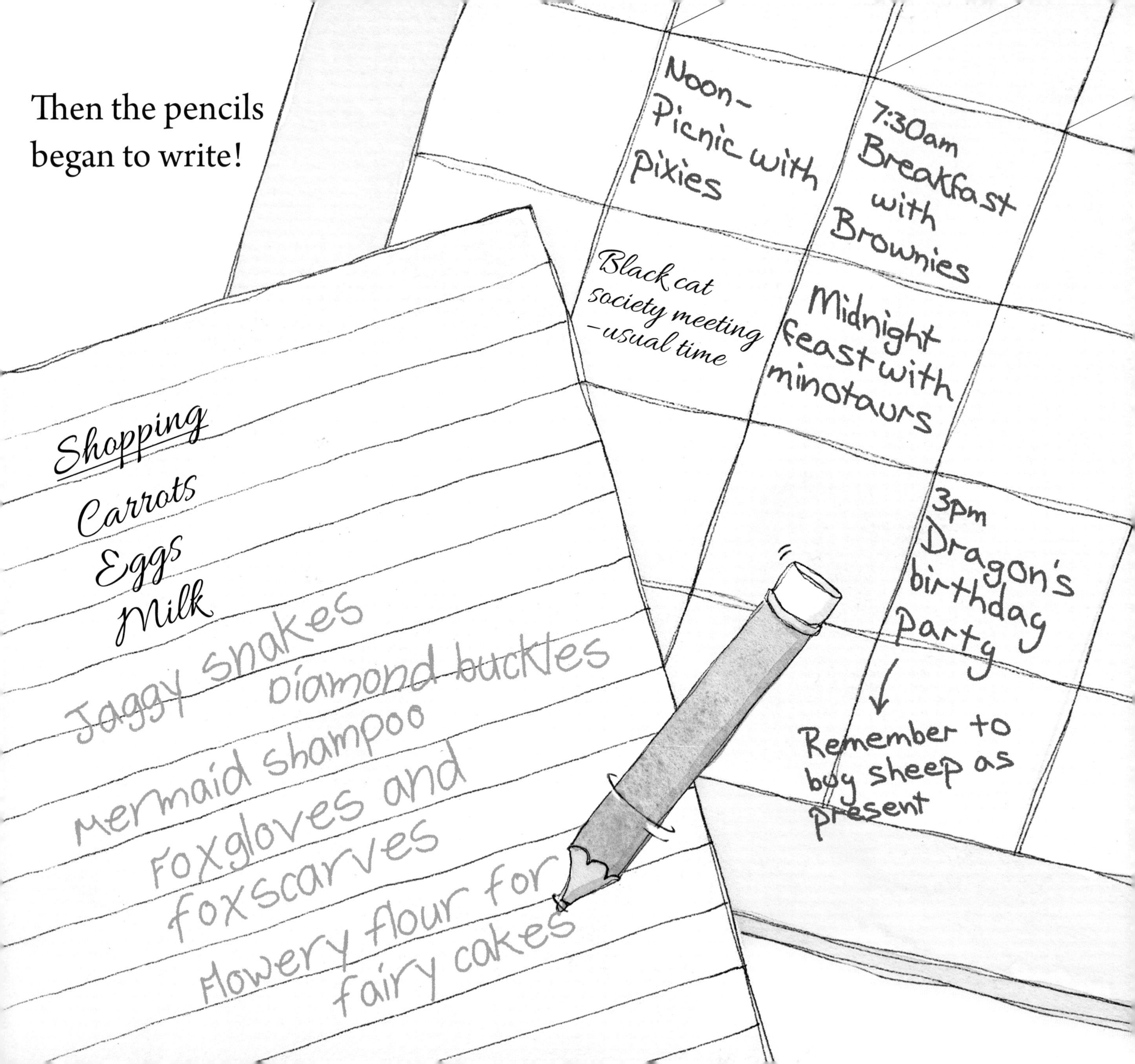

FRIDAY

SATURDAY

SUNDAY

Catriona's birthday

Catriona for the weekend

5pm Supper with sea monsters

VICTORIA SPONGE

Preparation time... 15–20 mins
Cooking time... approx. 20 mi
at 180°C

FOR THE CAKE

200g caster sugar
200g softened butter
4 eggs, beaten
200g self-raising
1 tsp baking pow
2 tbsp milk

For rainbow cake, mix with raindrops and bake in sunlight

FOR THE FILLING

100g butter, softened
140g icing sugar, sifted
few drops vanill

“No! Don’t do that!” gasped Catriona. “Write on the thank you letters instead!”

The pink pencil cartwheeled over to the table and scribbled on Auntie Annie’s letter:

"Oh no! That's rude!
Auntie Annie knitted
that hat herself.
Beanie, we've got to
catch these pencils!"

The pencils were drawing

faces on doorhandles,

sunrises on lampshades,

and footprints on the floor.

They drew a picnic on the table,

fairies flying on the ceiling,

and plants growing up the walls.

They were scribbling
too fast and bouncing
too high to catch.

So Catriona took a big
breath and shouted:

STOP,
PLEA

SEI!

The pencils stopped.

"Thank you," said Catriona. "You've drawn lovely pictures, but now it's time to tidy up.

So turn over onto your rubbery bottoms and rub everything out. *Please!*"

The pencils flipped over and rubbed everything out even faster than they had scribbled.

"Thank you so much. You must be tired after all that work. Why don't you have a lie down?" suggested Catriona.

She opened the pencil box and the pencils toppled in, then lay down. She closed the lid gently.

Catriona opened the cupboard door, and the cauldron and spoon danced back under the stairs.

Then Catriona sat down and used an ordinary school pencil to write her name neatly at the bottom of all her birthday thank you letters.

It didn't take nearly as long as she thought it would.

Aunt Griselda,
ou for the lovely books
ave me for my birthday.
ooking forward to reading
very one of them!
Love from,
Catriona
rs G. Whiteford
Rowan Cottage
Clovenshaws
TD21 3AB

The End